# moody road

## A NOVELLA

## CHRIS KAUZLARICH

PHANTOM QUILL
PRESS

 Formatted with Vellum

*For Kandice and Caleb.*
*May our minds be forever twisted.*

# moody road

I TRIED TO SWALLOW, the lump in my throat still a challenge to navigate. How does one get used to having no tongue—its remnants a knot of serrated tissue in my mouth, a clump of uneven flesh?

The memory of the blade slicing through the meat of it, the phantom pain still excruciating at times, was still fresh; really, the whole ordeal was.

I squeezed my eyes shut, trying to force away the images of that night that began flickering in my mind, panic beginning to rise as I felt the spit welling in my mouth.

I can do this.

I swallowed again, my throat flexing, forcing the mouthful of saliva down. I let out a breath. Everything was fine for now.

The jingling of keys captured my attention.

They're back. I hoped this would be it, the time I could finally convey my message, plead for my life, but I couldn't so much as turn my head to face the sound.

Patience. They'll unshackle me at some point. They had in the past to clean me, and also when I'd been allowed to feed myself—at least, that was before I used my utensil to try and cut my straps. Certainly, they would again.

I held my head still, something that wasn't too difficult considering my small range of motion, the current restraints akin to what held Hannibal Lecter in *The Silence of the Lambs.* My neck was stiff. It was overkill for somebody like me—I wasn't a threat, and I certainly never hurt anyone.

A man dressed all in black came into view and my heart sank. This wasn't my salvation. I'd seen men dressed like this before, and it usually meant pain. They were security toughs who were called if I even flicked an eyelash a way this place didn't like.

The man adjusted his shawl, and I saw a glimmer of white—it was a priest's collar—and my hopes rose almost instantly. I tried to lie more erect, a sign that I was at attention, eager. He set a bag down on the ground and rifled through it before sidling up beside me. He crossed himself, his lips moving in silent prayer. He held a notebook and a pen.

"Hello, my son," he said, face stoic. "We need to know what happened to you and to your friends before you came here. All of your families deserve to know. I am going to free your right hand so you can write, but remember, there are guards outside this room. This is your chance. Will you cooperate?"

I nodded as much as I could maneuver my head, thinking up prayers to a god I'd never believed in. I'd been tortured and mutilated, but maybe there was something to all of that if I could get out of here; if I could live.

The strap on my right wrist came free moments later, and the lack of pressure was immediate, like a deep breath after being trapped below water to my atrophied muscles and raw skin.

After I made a few flexes with my hand, the priest placed the pen between my fingers; I curled them around it. He then adjusted the bed so that I went from horizontal to vertical. Upright, with a side table in line with my hand. He nodded toward the notepad he'd placed there, the paper startingly white and empty, waiting for me to fill it with the ink of my memories.

I nodded, a wave of excitement taking hold as I began to write.

six months earlier

THE MOON WAS bright overhead as I slammed my car door, stepping out into the brisk autumn air. My cheeks and hands felt the bite as the wind blew through my friend's yard, his house nothing more than a small ranch and a pole barn a short drive down the road from a truck stop, the surrounding farm fields providing no obstruction to the noise or wind. At least I'd been forward-thinking enough to wear a thick hoodie as a layer, which kept my core warm.

I adjusted the beanie atop my head, pulling it down further to cover my ears, and proceeded to the house.

Gravel crunched underfoot as I walked, a sound so familiar I almost didn't hear it. We all grew up in the country, my family, my friends, and the constant sound of every movement on gravel, whether that be walking or driving down the road, was accompanied by dust clouds and pangs as the wheel wells were pelted—it was just par for the course. It was comfort. The only time something was amiss, worrying even, was when our version of white noise was disturbed. What a shock it had been to me when I started dating a guy in the next town over and he had a concrete driveway—the silence of it all.

I smiled though as the rocks shifted beneath my shoes, letting me know I was home. For some it may be odd, but to me, it was my solid footing.

*Crack!*

I whipped my head to the right, following the sharp noise that broke through the crunch. I knew I'd heard something, but as I looked on, my eyes could only make out shapes a few feet away, the orange glow of the porch light fading quickly into fragmented shapes of broken corn stalks that rolled on into the distance, the moonlight doing nothing more than casting shadows that made me feel like I was staring into a graveyard, jagged shapes abound—an ominous thought when we were about to visit a known haunted site. Or, at least, that's what the blog article that had popped up on my Facebook page claimed. Honestly, I hadn't read into it too deeply before sending it to my friends.

It was odd that I'd even come across it, really, I never used Facebook, but a week or so back, right after a bad breakup, I'd locked myself in my room for two days, essentially having a pity party of loneliness, obsessing over everyone else on my Instagram and TikTok posting videos and pictures of their happy lives and relationships. I knew social media was performative and often bullshit with its veneer of the good life, but I still let the algorithm take me for a ride of melancholy and self-loathing. It was then that I saw Sam and Lydia's picture together on her story, their wide smiles conveying a completeness that I'd never noticed before. It was different.

"They're fucking," I mumbled to myself, a flash of anger heating my cheeks. My two best friends in the whole world. I was happy for them if they were, truly, but it didn't lessen the sting of feeling utterly alone; that surge of betrayal that they were ruining something sacred, trying to erupt from its loosely contained well deep in my psyche.

*No, don't do that*, I thought, suppressing my resentments. What kind of friend was I if I let that feeling blossom, though my fear of Lydia taking Sam away from me wasn't new, the thought having always existed in one way or another.

I sighed and flipped to the Facebook app without thinking, needing to continue my numb scrolling despite the inconvenience of having to log on and everything. I started to browse.

"Moody Road?" I read aloud, as the blog post popped up, mentioning a haunted road not too far from where we lived. My mind went straight back to my best friends, the ones I'd just had a moment of jealousy with—they loved scary shit, especially Lydia. Checking out this so-called haunted road might be a perfect opportunity to hang out and break my foul post-breakup mood, plus I wanted to get to the bottom of my *they're fucking* theory.

*Crack!*

I jumped and scanned the field quickly again, my head zigzagging across the field. I needed to keep my mind on the present, or a coyote might jump out and get me, I thought, even though I knew that was probably bullshit. I felt extra jumpy, it seemed.

I wasn't old, a sprightly twenty-four, but I'd lived long enough, and in the country no less, through countless nights running through those fields. I even endured one tense summer when two escaped convicts roamed the area, hiding from police—they slept in the very pole barn just off to my left for one night, according to police. And even with all that, nothing had ever happened to make me question my safety or, for that matter, my spirituality, which, speaking plainly, was nonexistent. Hocus-pocus or ghosts or whatever somebody wanted to call them, didn't exist; it was as simple as that, so I needed to snap back to reality, back to my state of comfort in the environs I occupied.

I waited another moment before proceeding when nothing emerged. Logically speaking, it was probably just a loose stalk of corn snapping in the wind. I nodded as if that was settled and continued toward the house.

My suggestion to explore the haunted road worked and it was decided we'd make a night of it, like my friends wanted—I'd instigated it after all, piquing their interest with that damn blog, but it was also that time of year. If I weren't out with them seeking an instigator to my willies reflex, then I'd be at home, watching horror movies anyway. I might as well make it count.

The porch planks squeaked as I ascended and I flinched, the sound hearkening back to the stairs in my parents' house and the way I'd tried so hard to avoid those spots that would sound out, concealing my attempts to sneak boys up to my room in high school. I shuddered and cursed the psychology of my brain, the Pavlovian response to historical stimuli and trauma.

*Not today, Satan,* I thought, shrugging off the memories —my mental obstacles—and knocked on the front door.

The door flew open and two sets of arms reached out and enveloped me, squeezing tightly into a bear hug. I hardly had time to register the faces, but I already knew who held me: my safety net, my people, Sam and Lydia.

Sam and I had been thick as thieves since elementary school, no small feat for a lot of people, but much easier with our small country town, though that wasn't the only reason. He'd made it feel so natural, like us being friends was the most cherished pursuit in life. Lydia reinforced that commitment when she moved to town and joined our duo in middle school. Their personalities were simpatico with my own, as though they were but frag-ments of my psyche that somehow split from me at birth and formed into two people that would be my outward companions.

I told Sam all of this once, and he warned me I sounded a bit too spiritual, and I scoffed in return. It was nonsense; what I described to him was metaphysical and had nothing to do with the spiritual realm. His response was curt: "Stop using Wikipedia to look up definitions." Maybe he was right (I did do that).

Lydia pulled back first, leaning away to get a look at me while Sam and I still embraced. She smirked.

"You guys are so gay," she said and Sam released me, scowling in her direction.

"Nope, just Walker."

I shrugged. "We can't all be perfect, Sammy boy."

I hadn't always been so comfortable with myself and they both knew it, but their contented smiles let me know they recognized my progress, that steady emotional march I'd made toward self-acceptance.

"Speaking of which, I thought you were bringing a new boyfriend with you?" Lydia said.

My friends were happy that I'd found peace with who I was, but my inability to maintain a relationship still brought frowns. It was time to just rip off the Band-Aid.

"Sorry, Lyd, it didn't work out."

"Again? Wal—" She paused and held up her hand. "Sorry, I didn't mean to be judgy, I know that doesn't help. Are you okay?"

"Yeah, I'm good. We just weren't compatible."

"What are you looking for exactly, Walk? You go through guys like I go through tampons."

"Judging," I said in response as Sam said, "Ew, gross."

Lydia gave me a bashful shrug before training her gaze on Sam, eyes narrowing.

"Oh shut up, Sam. Women menstruate. If you can't handle that, then you'll always be single."

I had to consciously remember not to roll my eyes. And I confirmed they were fucking—Sam's little grin revealed it all.

"Seriously, though, Walk, what happened with this one? You're going to run out of options, or at least ones that aren't closeted hillbillies, really soon. Have you forgotten we live in the middle of nowhere? Dating apps don't reach the city with us being this far out, or at least I don't think people set their radius that far."

"That's the key, Lyd. There are closets full of hypocrites all over the apps locally."

Her eyes widened, mouth pulling back in disgust. I couldn't keep a straight face.

"As if! I'm not that desperate. That is part of the problem, though. I've had to go downtown to Chicago for dates, and once they find out I live an hour and a half away in rural Indiana, they pull the plug. I've had to settle for trying to pull off one-night stands because that's as far as it will go."

Sam scoffed. "That's more than I'm getting."

The tone of his voice wasn't very convincing.

"I thought your hand looked like it'd been rubbed raw," Lydia said.

"Fuck off," he replied, smiling, his stare lingering.

Despite their poorly concealed relationship, I'd missed this banter with my friends. I had been so preoccupied lately with looking to get away from the expanse of nothingness we lived in that I'd neglected them. I wished I could be content like they were, but maybe I just needed to try to be okay with not having a relationship. What was it that people always said? "It will happen when you least expect it"? Of course, that was easier for straight couples, and my dear friends had each other.

I wished they would just tell me so I didn't have to keep dwelling on it. That night should be a perfect opportunity.

"Come on in, buddy," Sam said, and they entered the living room. The warmth was immediate, and not just the temperature. The space was rife with nostalgia from our youth: the worn beige sofa, the shag carpeting discolored from one too many spills, and the oversized LCD TV, far too big for the space, with its cords strewn about, running from the wall and connecting numerous gaming consoles.

I sat down, sinking into the broken in cushions like I always had. Lydia plopped down next to me, wasting no time in laying out a map of northern Indiana.

"What's this for?"

"To find Moody Road."

"I thought you knew where it was. Besides, we do live in the modern age, Lyd," I said, raising my smartphone out in front of me and giving it a little shake.

She rolled her eyes. "We have a general idea of the location, but the blogs say there is no cellular service because, for one, it's in the middle of a field with no other homes or towns close by, and two, well, it's paranormal."

"Yeah, okay, fine."

Lydia stared at me, expectant. "Didn't you read the links I texted to you?"

I shrugged, smiling sheepishly.

"Walker Herbert, how could you?" she said playfully. I held up my middle finger prominently in her face; I wanted to make sure there was no missing it.

She knew how to push my buttons, and if there was one thing that depressed them fully, it was hearing my full name thrown about—that daily reminder of my dad's insistence on patriotism after 9/11, even though naming me after George W. Bush would have made more sense to me than after Bush Sr., but my dad wasn't a logical man. I guess I should just be glad my name wasn't George.

Lydia swatted my hand. "I trusted that you and Sam had this handled."

"Wow, I wish everyone had this level of confidence in us. Imagine the kind of world we'd live in."

"Don't put that juju on me; I have a hard enough time falling asleep at night," Sam said, reentering the room and slamming a backpack down on the floor. It made a loud *clunk*.

"Haha," Lydia mocked, but her expression held a glimmer again. Those two were beginning to make me a little sick—goddamn their cuteness. I needed to get this out of them so I could openly be happy for them. Well, at least when I wasn't feeling jealous, which I had to admit nagged at me just a bit.

"What you got there?" I asked, nudging the bag with my foot.

"That there, my friend, is some provisions."

"Provisions? Where the hell are the two of you taking me?"

"Oh, calm down, it's only an hour or so away. But we aren't sure if the phenomenon happens right away or if you need to wait around a bit, so we packed a few bottles of water, some soda, snacks; you know, essentials."

"Essentials for a car ride? What are you, a soccer mom?"

"Fine then, Walk, don't have any, but we all know how much of a bitch you are when you're hangry," Sam said, sitting on the armrest nearest Lydia.

"Since you read all about it, what are we supposed to

see, anyway? When I saw the blog post, I really only read the haunted road part before sending it to you."

Lydia's eyes widened, not in surprise, but excitement. She lived for horror stuff and I knew then she'd been waiting for me to give her an opening to download what she learned, her forehead already scrunching with determination.

"Lights!"

I frowned. "Lights?"

"Yes, well, a light, but not just any light; it is a globe of fire, or so it's been described, that travels down the road toward you, drawing nearer until—" She paused, her face contorting as she searched for words.

"Until what?"

"Until it just vanishes."

"That's awfully anticlimactic," I said.

"Okay, but there has to be more to it than that. Where does it come from? After it vanishes, what happens? Something has to happen, Walk."

"And we intend to find out," Sam said, patting her shoulder.

"Uh-huh," I said, feeling as though I just sat through a hype speech in a movie (cue the triumphant music). "So the provisions are in case it takes a while, is what you're telling me."

"Bingo," Sam said. "First, to get it to work, we have to flash our high beams from the side of the road closest to the old house that is there, and then, once finished, we have to turn our headlights off. From what we've read, the phenomenon occurs soon after. Everyone leaves once they've seen it, describing it as eerie but with no explanation. We want to be the first to document the aftermath— to find that explanation."

I nodded. I didn't have the heart to tell them this sounded like a complete waste of time, their evident excitement being just enough to temper my default pessimism. Besides, this sounded like the kind of wild goose chase we used to have in high school—again with the nostalgia. I either did this with them, or I sat at home playing video games before breaking down and opening a dating app where I would swipe left or right for hours until I inevitably got frustrated, beat off, and passed out. Hanging with my two best friends seemed the best choice.

"And you know what, Sam-o? I think we need to be the ones who discover that answer."

"Hell yes," Sam said, giving me a playful pat on the arm. Lydia was also beaming with excitement.

"Let's go!" Sam said, hopping to his feet and slinging the backpack over his shoulder, fist raised in the air triumphantly. He looked like Mario after completing a level in any number of the iconic Nintendo games. "I'll warm up the truck."

I exchanged an amused glance with Lydia before also getting to my feet. She folded her map and slid it into her pocket, and I extended my hand toward the door.

"After you."

*ii*

"TURN HERE," Lydia said from her position riding shotgun in Sam's truck, huddled over the map, the bright beam of her cell phone flashlight illuminating the worn paper. She was like a general inspecting a battlefield.

"Are you sure? That doesn't look like a road."

"Sam, are you driving or navigating?"

Sam's mouth clenched shut, his jaw set and stiff, but he didn't respond, obeying her command. The truck lurched as we turned off the paved county road onto a single-lane path that didn't even appear to be graveled, with large, murky divots littering our way forward.

I could see Lydia's face in the visor mirror from where I sat in the backseat, a guilty scrunching of her forehead each time we hit a bump that would have had us airborne if not for the seatbelts holding us in place.

I pivoted back and forth, trying to see outside from my position with limited visibility, hoping to spot an exit to this torturous road, but we were in some kind of trench, with earthen mounds on either side of the road that were close to the height of the truck. My palms started to sweat.

"Hey Lyd, do you happen to know how much long-ER?" I asked, my voice rising in a burst of volume as we hit another bump.

She shook her head and gave me a meek smile in the mirror.

"We're almost there. Sorry about this, Walk."

Sam remained silent, eyes fixed on the road ahead. He was pissed and likely wondering where his apology was—it was his truck getting beaten to hell, after all.

We continued for another minute or so before Lydia tensed, sitting more erect and yelling, "Turn right!"

Sam did so, the tires squealing as we performed a quick S-curve onto a wider gravel road, the earthen mounds no longer boxing us in, revealing field after field of dying corn husks.

"I have to ask...This ball of flame—what's the lore behind it?"

"I sent—Nevermind, I forgot you didn't read what I texted you."

I rolled my eyes. "You know how I feel about required reading, Lyd."

She turned around in her seat, her expression like that of a teacher exasperated by the ignorance of a pupil, and prepared to give yet another lecture. She leaned in closer to me, her head even with her seat's headrest.

"Don't get snippy, Walk. Now, Moody Road is a local legend about a man named Mr. Moody. I don't know his first name, but I don't think that's important. He had something happen to his family, something bad, and they named the street after where he lived and, to this day, haunts.

"To give you a little background, the inciting incident happened a long time ago, when homes were spread far and wide, much more so than they are now. I'm talking where a person might not see a neighbor for miles and miles."

I looked out the window as Lydia spoke, at the empty fields surrounding us. How was it any different now?

"Mr. Moody was a farmer, but he had to travel into town on business from time to time. Unfortunately, they couldn't just make a call or drive thirty minutes as we can now; he had to load up his wagon and set off on a multi-hour journey that resulted in an overnight stay before heading home. He was called to town, and, as usual, he left his wife, children, and maid to tend to the farm.

"It is said that on this particular trip, Mr. Moody left before dawn, hoping that he could be back that night since there were just too many chores needing doing for him to stay away an entire day. And, true to his word, he returned that evening, hours past nightfall. He entered his house, hoping for a hot meal after such travels, only to find his family brutally murdered, their bodies mutilated, entrails scattered all about, and the maid's remains nowhere to be seen."

Lydia had my full attention, our eyes locked on one another as she recited the tale, a feeling of dread seeping ever further into my bones. This is what she and Sam wanted to find? A ghostly light at the scene of such evil? I wanted to tell her to stop, to tell them to turn the car around, but I was entranced, desperately convincing myself it was all just a story. Surely if this were true, it'd be more commonly known.

Lydia continued.

"The police came from town the next day and search parties dispersed amongst the fields and local area, looking for someone untoward that could be hiding, as nobody in this community would do such a thing, but their efforts amounted to nothing. Mr. Moody became obsessive and deranged, stalking out into the night, muttering to himself and searching with just his lantern, never giving up hope. Locals reported seeing that twinkle of his lantern from their windows at all hours, as if he didn't sleep, stalking the darkness alone.

"After months of this, and with the police no closer to finding the killer or the whereabouts of the missing maid, Mr. Moody hung himself from a tree downfield from his home, his mad mutterings all but consuming him and making him the community pariah. It is said that the ball of light that's seen outside his house is Old Man Moody, returning to seek vengeance on the trespasser who took his family from him."

Lydia stopped speaking, breathless after her recital of the story, a glow of excitement reddening her cheeks. It was in direct contrast to the chill that penetrated my skin, burrowing just beneath the surface, refusing to be dislodged despite the truck's heat being on full blast. Goosebumps flourished along my arms and legs and I clenched my jaw to prevent my teeth from chattering. How could she be excited about this expedition?

"Let me get this straight," I started, battling my anxiety for dominance, for control. "You want to antagonize a ghost by flashing our headlights at it so it flies down the road and hunts us?"

Lydia pulled back, treating my incredulity like a slap.

"Come on, Walker. You have always been Mr. This-Shit-Isn't-Real. Besides, there are blogs, Facebook pages, and websites dedicated to the paranormal where people have shared their accounts of going. None of them references any harm coming to them. We'll be fine," Sam said, coming to Lydia's defense; any sign of his earlier annoyance evaporated.

"Be that as it may, you've said those other people left after they saw Moody's light. They didn't stick around with a bag of snacks, hoping to see Old Man Moody apparate right before them with his lantern, and who knows what kind of weapon, in hand."

"You're taking this a bit far, Walk. We aren't hoping to see him with a weapon. I thought we were all in agreement that we wanted to see what actually caused the light, and knew that the lore was just that—a folk tale. You don't actually believe we are in danger, do you?" Lydia asked.

I stopped short. My typical response would be to scoff and roll my eyes at this whole endeavor, but a sheen of dread as thin as the morning dew clung to me; her story had only made the sensation stickier.

I hated her then, for the span of a breath, almost like something else took hold of me, trying to pit me against her: for the invalidation, for the shaming. First, she took my best friend away, seducing him, and now this? A roiling of anger blossomed in my core before I realized where I'd let my thoughts go and saw the ludicrousness of it all, and a stab of guilt replaced it.

*What the hell was that? What's wrong with me?* Lydia was one of my best friends; she didn't mean anything by what she said. She was right about my response; that is how I thought and acted.

I gave my head a shake, as if I could fling the thoughts away, and forced myself to swallow, trying to moisten my dry throat.

"I guess not. I'm being silly."

"That's the spirit!" Lydia said, facing forward in her seat, her cheery disposition doing nothing to quell my unease.

We continued on in silence for a time, the fields stretching on for miles without a single reprieve from the dark, the only twinkle being from the stars above. After twenty minutes, much of the enthusiasm that previously permeated from Sam and Lydia seemed to have evaporated.

I watched her, wondering what she was thinking as she

peered out the window at the endless nothingness cruising past us, when she started suddenly. She'd seen something.

"What is it?"

"Hold on, Walk. Sam, slow down. I think that's a silo out there," she said, turning on her flashlight and looking at her map.

I frowned, searching the blackness out of the windshield. I could faintly see the moon's glow casting an outline on a structure a few hundred feet away.

"That isn't remarkable, Lyd. There are probably hundreds of silos out there. We're surrounded by fields."

"We are, yes, but that one is our landmark. From what I read, we should see it from the road in this general vicinity. Sam, is that route 49 on your left?"

"Sure looks like it," Sam said, looking to the pinpricks of light a few miles in the distance that Lydia was pointing to. She smiled broadly, the excitement returning to her face in a flush of color.

"Bingo! That means—Sam, turn here—that we've arrived."

Sam followed her directions, taking a right onto the small side road that led out into an unlit field, the shadows of structures faintly visible in the spotty moonlight.

"How far do we go?"

"It isn't much further, Sam. Loop around until we reach—Oh shit, look, there's the silo again! We're almost there." Lydia could hardly contain her excitement, practically rocking in her seat.

I looked out the passenger-side window, and there, in the ever-diminishing distance, was the silo, its structure pockmarked and jagged like a mountain peak, its conical top slanted at a precarious angle. I had no idea how it still stood.

We drew closer, the truck moving at a steady clip, until we finally passed under its shadow. I shuddered as the darkness swallowed our vehicle, if only for a moment. My breath caught, and I counted the seconds as the imposing form blotted out the moon. I couldn't say why; it must have been that ever-lurking skein of dread that managed to twist its way around my heart, cinching it with each new malevolent possibility that had crossed my mind on our little journey.

The newest knot formed as I glimpsed a gaping hole in the silo's side, the shadowed interior leaving my mind racing with thoughts of unseen phantoms watching us from within.

*It will pass, it will pass*, I repeated in my mind as a mantra while waiting for the moon's pale rays to return. It was then that I felt the sting of loneliness once more, my hand itching to reach out and cling to someone for reassurance, my age-old need and insecurities rearing their ugly heads like the Gorgon's fateful curse.

Intellectually, I knew I was with my friends who radiated their companionable love to me since our youth, but they had something between them that I didn't. Theirs was a special love, like that extra layer of cozy blanket on a cold winter morning, when all I had was the sheet; sure, it provided a covering to hold to, but my body's heat dissipated all the same. I loved them so much, yet my heart yearned for something more; why couldn't I have it, too?

Resentment fueled the turn of my head as I focused on them, on the twitch of their fingers as they drew closer to one another on the center armrest, before remembering themselves in front of me, so as not to give away their secret.

*Oh, just fucking do it. Just—*

I flinched, surprised by the venom lacing my thoughts. I shook my head, banishing the thoughts that seemed to be growing a bit too comfortable in my head. I would not resent my friends.

I crossed my arms around my chest—I'd been giving myself hugs since 2001—willing away the chill and dark clouds spiraling in my head. I rubbed my hands against my biceps, the friction causing the faintest hints of warmth to blossom along their path.

"Just a little farther," Lydia said.

A lone tree was next, tall and stately in contrast to the silo we'd just passed, a testament to nature's ability to endure while our manmade structures had their shelf life. I wondered if that was the tree Lydia told me about, the one Mr. Moody decided to end it all from, dangling in a noose. A house materialized moments later, two hundred feet or so from the tree, all but confirming my suspicions. I felt my pulse quicken.

"That house...Is it *the* house? Mr. Moody's?" I asked.

"Yeah," Lydia said, her voice quiet. At first, I thought it was reverence, but her visor was still down, and her face, reflected in the mirror, looked confused.

"I would have thought it'd have been knocked down or, if anything, renovated, but that house, it looks so—"

"Old," Sam finished for her, his voice sounding just as wary as Lydia's.

I understood the sentiment and wondered if they were thinking what I was: Does someone live there? That was ridiculous, I knew—based on the level of disrepair, with the home's condition matching that of the silo, certainly it had to be condemned—but the thought of someone or something peering out at us from its windows was unshakable.

I waited for a shifting shadow or for a light to flicker on

in one of the upper-floor windows, breath held, but everything remained as it was. The only movement being that of a single shutter, barely attached by a lone hinge, swaying in the breeze, its gentle tapping as it hit the side of the house the only noise in the night. It made my heart stutter.

We passed the house. One hundred feet, then two hundred—then Sam came to a stop.

"Did you see anything?" He asked, both hands on the steering wheel.

"Nothing," I replied.

"It is a bit creepy in the dark, isn't it?"

"That's an understatement, Lyd. So now what?" I asked.

"To see the light, we're supposed to turn around to face the way we came and flash our headlights three times. Sam?"

He flinched like he'd been startled. "Hmm? Sorry, what did you say?"

"You need to turn the truck around. Is everything alright?"

He met her gaze. "Yeah, I thought I saw something move out there. It was nothing. My mind must be playing tricks on me."

The three of us peered out the windows again; nothing moved but the gentle swaying of the remaining corn stalks shifting in the breeze under the faint moonlight.

"Just the wind, right? Nothing to worry about. Let's do this, huh?" Sam asked, but his voice lacked conviction.

He put the truck in reverse and repositioned it so we were facing the house again, the tree and silo further out in the distance.

Sam flashed his high beams three times and turned off his headlights. We plunged into a landscape of shadows.

I could hear my heart beating, the rhythm faster than it

should be. That wouldn't do; I couldn't just listen to myself spiral into a state of anxiety lest panic would take hold.

"I have a question. Why do all of these folktales require doing things three times? What is three times doing that once doesn't? Is the ghost just sitting around when he sees a flash or two and says, 'Just two flashes? They aren't serious?' Better yet, three times for Candyman, Bloody Mary, or even Chucky Mudd—like, what gives?"

Lydia and Sam both faced me, their expressions opposites: hers amused, his incredulous.

"Somebody trying to distract themself much?"

I smirked. Lydia knew me too well. Anytime I got uncomfortable, not wanting to face the situation at hand, I'd resort to sarcastic humor or distraction—"Hey, look over there: a squirrel!"

Sam shook his head, facing forward. "I think we need to keep our focus on our surroundings...quietly."

"Oh, come on, Sam. What are you—?"

"Shh, look!" Sam said, interrupting me and pointing toward the distance. I looked where he indicated and saw there was a glimmer of light, much like the glare when the sun reflects off a mirror.

A wave of relief flooded every cavity of my consciousness. I couldn't believe I'd been so foolish. Anticipation of this little flicker was what had me all out of sorts. I grinned, looking from Lydia then to Sam, but they were transfixed. Couldn't they see how absurd this all was?

"You know what this is, right? It's so obvious. It's just headlights from route 49. Mystery solved," I said, still watching the light, which moved closer, ever so slowly.

"Nah, Walker, this isn't that. Route 49 is that way," Sam said, pointing just to the right of the ball of light.

I followed the angle of Sam's finger, about thirty

degrees, and caught the fading red of taillights. My head whipped back to Moody's light; it flickered like a flame, hues of orange becoming distinct.

"Maybe it's another car coming?"

"With just a single headlight and that color to boot? What are the odds? No, Walk, this is the Moody light; Old Man Moody's spirit looking for his family's killer," Lydia said, her voice breathy. She sounded calm, trance-like.

"Then his search will end at us," I whispered.

Sam grunted in reply, but he didn't move. There was no burst into action, the adrenaline-fueled self-preservation one would expect from such a confirmation. But it wasn't just him and Lydia. As much as I flailed internally, my brain scrambling for action—to pull open the car door and run, or to knock Sam out of the way to commandeer the truck and flee—I did nothing. I was fixed to my spot in the back-seat, eyes glued to the fiery orb that had grown to the size of a Labrador.

"It's getting closer." Lydia started, her voice becoming high-pitched and squeaky. "Maybe we should—" but her words cut off, seemingly lodged in her throat. She was finally showing fear, but it wasn't enough to break the hold the paranormal light had over us; none of us moved.

The light seemed to pick up speed in approaching us, or it grew at an accelerated rate; I couldn't tell which, as I couldn't discern actual movement, but it had become the size of a Mini Cooper. The shock subsided and I regained enough of my self-control to look to the left at the house and the tree. Both were still cloaked in darkness. Certainly the amount of light emitted by that ball of fire should've illuminated them like the Fourth of July, projecting shadows all over the long stretch of lawn between them, but there was only that same ghostly light of the moon.

"Oh my God! Sam!" Lydia shouted, and I caught her grasping his hand. The Moody light had grown to nearly the size of a school bus, blocking the entire road we were parked on.

"I've got you," he said back to her.

But who had me? My heart was sprinting, nearly beating out of my chest as my breath reached the cusp of hyperventilation. *Goddamn them*, I thought resentfully. But it wasn't possible to dwell on my feelings; survival mattered more.

I acted, my limbs moving automatically, as instinct finally tunneled to the surface and took control. I unbuckled, leaned over the center console, reached over Sam, steadied myself on the steering wheel, and turned the key in the ignition.

*iii*

"HEY," Sam yelled, startled by my quick movements as the truck started, the engine's initial rev like the roar of a lion. The eerie silence of watching death race toward us was shattered by the sustained rumble of the idling diesel engine, and it was as if all three of us woke from a shared dream as the truck's headlights flashed into being. It all happened in rapid succession, a domino effect that completed its circuit in mere seconds; we'd hardly been able to process it. The Moody light was gone.

Sam cleared his throat and gave me a nudge with his shoulder. I was draped across his and Lydia's hands, pinning them down with my crotch. I retreated back to my seat but raised an eyebrow at their hands; Sam averted his gaze. Lydia was already looking elsewhere, searching.

The night was as still and calm as it had been before we'd flashed our lights, summoning Moody's ghost.

"Where did it go?" Sam asked.

Lydia shrugged. "Who knows, but go! We have to see what happened to the road; look for burns or remnants."

"Okay, okay, no need to shout," he said, throwing the truck into drive and mashing the accelerator.

I flinched as rocks kicked up from the spinning tires, the truck lurching forward once it found traction. I was happy for the movement, the ending of us sitting there like lambs to the slaughter, but there was still a lingering fear hovering over me; a fear of drawing attention to ourselves, which we'd done enough of already. That light, whatever it was, was certainly seeking out something.

"What happened to the bloggers who've come here before? Did they wait out the light or get freaked like me and start their cars too?"

Lydia shook her head. "I really don't know, Walk. It never said. I just assumed the Moody light stopped and they went on their way, but after this," she waved her hand before her, encompassing the dark expanse around them, "I can't imagine they sat there patiently until the end."

I nodded in silent agreement and focused on the road. It looked the way it had when the light first appeared: weathered but untouched by the ball's flames that we assumed would have licked its surface.

We started to approach the tree on our left, that lone obstruction between the house and the silo, and I glanced at it, almost dismissively, as my eyes swept across that stretch of the land, when a shadow caught my attention.

*What was that?*

I retraced the path, squinting to identify what I'd caught in the previously lit landscape that had fallen dark as the headlight beams moved forward, when I saw a shifting of shadow, like a globe tilting on its axis, against the tree. It almost resembled—

"Stop the car!"

Sam slammed on the brakes, and I flew forward, catching myself on their seats to prevent myself from flying into the dashboard.

"Jesus, Walk, what is it?" Sam asked, looking at me.

"Over there." I pointed at the tree. "The shadow."

"What shadow?" Lydia asked, leaning over Sam to peer out the driver's side window.

The tree was darker than it had been, a blanket of cloud

cover having moved into place, blocking the moon's already limited glow. I sighed.

"I don't see anything. What do you think you saw?"

"A body dangling from a noose."

The truck was quiet for several moments as my words sank in.

Sam scoffed. "Alright, I call bullshit. Stop trying to freak us out, Walk."

"I'm not bullshitting, Sam. There was a body, or something, hanging from that tree, or at least the shadow of something. Er, well, anyway, it was large, okay. I know what I saw."

"And now it's gone. But look, Sam, I think considering what we've already seen, we can all agree that anything is possible, right?" Lydia asked.

He nodded reluctantly, his forehead scrunched. I knew it wasn't that Sam didn't believe me, it was that he didn't want to. He knew the indications of what I'd seen meant as far as what the light really was. The ghost hunter idea was a lot more appealing when the possibility seemed, well, impossible.

"I don't know about you guys, but I certainly want to know what all this means, and we didn't drive all the way out here to just fuck off right away at the first sight of something unnerving. We said we'd look around and try to figure this out, and I still intend to."

Sam and I looked at one another. I could see the hesitancy in his eyes.

Lydia didn't wait for us—true to her word, she opened the truck door and hopped out.

"What the fuck? Lyd!" Sam said, opening his door and following her as she made her way around the truck and started across the field toward the tree.

It amazed me how much we'd all changed over the years. In middle and high school I was the reckless one; the angry gay kid with the devil-may-care attitude, looking for that next high or danger, never caring what happened to me. It was unsurprising that I was the target for all the assholes with their toxic little egos, all because I made the mistake of kissing the wrong boy at a party in eighth grade. He was into it until another friend walked in on us, exposing my sexuality, which I was just beginning to discover, to the world. He denied his part, of course, and I became the fag who "assaulted" him. I was then a pariah to all but Sam and, eventually, Lydia, who moved to town a few months later.

From then on, Sam and Lydia always tried to rein me in, up until senior year, when I met a guy at another school, which initiated my first real relationship. It's like with me taking life more seriously now we'd switched places, and Lydia had become the thrill seeker.

*And there she goes, acting as reckless as I once did*, I thought as I watched the flashlight beams from their cellphones bounce along the grass and faintly light the tree. There was no hanging body there—at least, not anymore.

"I should probably join them," I muttered, but I didn't want to. It was dark on either side of the truck, and I could see the subtle movements of the corn stalks in the field. A fear of the unseen watcher I'd sensed before nagged at me. It caused me to itch, a tickle between my shoulder blades that flitted downward like a hair stuck on the inside of a staticky shirt, rubbing against my skin, instigating shivers and goosebumps.

"Fuck this." I opened the driver's side passenger door, stepping out into the chilly night. "Hey, wait up!"

They circled the tree, their beams of light spiraling

around it under the moonless sky, making them stand out that much more in the dark. If only the cloud cover could have been held at bay for a bit longer; its entrance added to that ominous itch flitting along my back.

I ran. I nearly tripped several times on the uneven ground, struggling to focus on the objective at hand: just reach my friends.

I heard a snap, a sound like dry twigs underfoot, but my path was clear. Maybe it was the corn stalks off to my left. I stopped and scanned the field, my breath caught in my throat. I couldn't see anything but those unseen eyes; I could feel the heat of them on me like the unwelcome groping of a stranger, cupping and prodding.

"Walk?"

I screamed as Lydia said my name, her voice next to my right ear, and spun to face her. She dropped her phone, and it landed flashlight up, illuminating her from below. She was clutching her chest, her features cast in a ghoulish pallor.

"Jesus, why are you screaming?"

"Because you scared the shit out of me!"

"Well, sorry, I didn't mean to. Shit, Walk."

I waved her off, catching my breath as she bent over to retrieve her phone.

"Did you see anything at the tree?" I asked.

"No, it just looked like a tree. No sign of scratches, missing bark, ropes, nothing. What were you looking at, anyway?"

I faced away from her toward the field, but the night was as still and dark as it had been before.

"I thought I heard something when I was running toward you from the truck."

"Probably just your imagination playing tricks. I know mine is running wild being out here," Sam said, joining us.

As much as I hated the accusation—not the first lobbed at me that night, as if I was a delicate flower who couldn't handle the situation—I knew that Sam was probably right. I was reading into every shadow, every caress of the wind more than I should have been. It wasn't Sam's fault for trying to point that out; it was his way of soothing me, feeling invalidated was my problem, my trauma.

*Just chill.*

"I suppose you're right," I said, my tone anything but convincing. "I have this feeling, though, this tickle on my neck, that sixth-sense feeling of being watched. Do you know what I mean?"

"Yeah, I do," Sam said, looking around. "I don't see where someone could hide if they were watching us, though, Walk."

"Are you serious right now? Look around, Sam. The cloud cover has made this whole area a perfect hiding spot. I can't distinguish a person squatting down out there from the corn stalks littering the area. And what about the house and the silo? Who knows what could be lurking in those?"

*Smack.*

*Smack.*

*Smack.*

The house's dangling shutter flapped in the breeze, drawing our attention; its sound pierced the night like a howl in a crypt, dreadful and unexpected.

My breath caught, thoughts of Edgar Allan Poe's "The Tell-Tale Heart" and "The Fall of the House of Usher" swimming in my head, fear seizing on the opportunity, threatening to fill my lungs.

Sam and Lydia trained their phones on the looming

house, lighting up sections of chipped siding and missing shingles, the paint nearly gone from decades of abandonment and harsh winters. The shadows stretching across its outer walls didn't match its topography, morphing into jagged shapes like black fire instead of clean roof and window lines.

"Pretty creepy, huh?" Lydia asked.

"Mhmm," I muttered. "I don't like the vibe. Something isn't right."

"Let's move over to the silo. I don't want to stay out here much longer. I'm perfectly fine to admit that I'm starting to get scared a little shitless," Sam said.

A strong gust of wind came from the northwest, piercing through my clothing like an icicle through a soft layer of snow. A spasm rocked me, the likes I'd only felt after falling through the ice and into frigid water when I was young.

Lydia and Sam locked eyes with me, their bodies doing a similar jig as mine. We needed to leave.

"Jesus! It's fucking freezing. I'm going back to the truck," Sam bit out between chattering teeth.

Lydia nodded in agreement, her eyes wide. Her eagerness had been quashed; I could see it plainly in the pale tint of her cheeks.

*Snap!*

We ran at the sound, not one of us looking behind us to investigate. We were like the gazelles on the great African plain, running for our lives from the lion hiding in the brush, our feet seeming to sail over the grass. We didn't embody the horror movie trope where one of us fell. A divine hand was moving us forward on puppet strings, or so it seemed.

I reached the truck first, lunging into the backseat with

such momentum that I slid across into the door opposite. I rubbed my arm as I rocked back and forth.

*Come on, come on, come on!*

Sam and Lydia hopped in and slammed the doors. A forceful clink reverberated through the cabin like a gunshot as the door lock pins bolted into their engaged position.

I exhaled.

"I'm assuming you heard the noise this time?"

"Fuck off, Walk," Lydia said, but there was no heat in it. She sounded as drained as I felt.

I'd be lying if I said I didn't want to floor it out of there and say screw it to the whole Moody Road adventure, but I bit my tongue; something held me back. A strange sense of satisfaction simmered in my core. Was it because we were safe in the car, nothing having happened to us other than a cold gust of wind and the snapping of kindling out in the field? That had to be it; we had hardly been in danger, no matter what my imagination and 150-beats-per-minute heart rate were telling me.

*Yes,* I told myself, *we're good,* though the feeling in my gut still felt wrong.

I snapped back to the present and saw Lydia was staring at me. A spike of malice wormed its way up my throat, rebuffing her judgment.

*Who does she think she is? She steals my best friend away from me and then dares to—* I gasped.

"Are you okay?" I heard her ask me.

I nodded, forcing down the sensations trying to boil over. *What the fuck is wrong with me? Lydia is my friend too. She loves me.*

"Okay, well, since we've had a moment to catch our breath," Lydia said, "I've noticed nothing happened. I think we are just a bit jumpy out here in the dark with no cellular service, but the night is just playing tricks on us. I still want to check out the silo. We came all this way; it would be silly not to.

"I know what we saw, and there has to be an explanation for the light. Look at how many people were on the blog talking about seeing it. They all made it home. I never once read anything about any disappearances."

"Except for the maid," I said, and she shrugged.

"Well, yeah, except her."

"Lyd, are we sure about that? Did you even look to see if there had been any missing persons in the news?" Sam asked, and Lydia's cheeks reddened.

I tingled with contentment. *That's it, you tell her, Sammy. He's not totally under your thumb, is he, Lydia?*

"Let's just do it, Sam. It's literally on the way out of here, anyway."

"I vote no, Lyd," I said.

Sam furrowed his brow, and I could see the indecision on his face. He looked at me, then to Lydia, and then back again. Poor Sam. Not only was he caught between friends, but now he was caught between his best friend and his girlfriend.

*That bitch was trying to*—Why was I thinking this way? I clenched my eyes shut, trying to clear my mind, purge my psyche of the toxic stinger poisoning me against Lydia.

*Stop!* They both deserved happiness; not everything revolved around me.

I looked at Sam again; his face was still scrunched.

*Why not stay and see what this is all about—what could it hurt?* I felt a cramp, a stab of worry at that thought; it felt as alien to me as the flares of resentment.

I let out a sigh. "We might as well."

Sam's eyebrows shot up in surprise. "Yeah, alright. If

you're both sure," he said, and Lydia gave a wan smile as if she wasn't so sure of what she'd asked of us.

"Okay, yes. Let's do this," she said in response.

Sam smiled and nodded at me. Despite my unease, I couldn't help but stifle a giggle as I pictured the meme of all the actors nodding encouragement to one another, starting with Sir Michael Caine. Sam gave me a quizzical look, then turned forward and started the truck.

"Are you laughing?" Lydia asked.

"No, just nervous that we're going to die. No big deal."

"Oh my God, Walk, don't curse us!"

I flashed a cheesy grin, and Lydia narrowed her eyes at me in the visor mirror before flipping it up. My stomach churned as the truck lurched forward.

The silo wasn't far, a few hundred feet at best, but Sam crept the truck forward as if afraid he'd miss a turn or something. It reminded me of what Dane Cook said in one of his old comedy bits: "Just follow the one fucking road you're on to me," with, in our case, the silo being the "me." I still couldn't believe that jagged metal structure still stood.

Sam put the truck in park. "Ready?"

Lydia and I both nodded.

"Let's get this over with," I said.

I turned on my phone's flashlight and exited the truck. I worried about the device's battery, especially with how uncertain I felt, but I hoped this final trek wouldn't take long. We'd go into the silo, do a quick scan, and get the hell out of there. Easy-peasy.

"Watch your step," Sam called out after he'd stepped over a serrated shard of metal, a point where the siding had shorn off from the exterior, allowing access to the structure's innards. *What could have created the hole?* I wondered, inspecting the opening as I prepared to pass through, the edges as rough as a piece of paper after a four-year-old went at it with a pair of dull scissors. I shivered again and stepped inside.

After crossing the threshold, it was like I'd been transported to another world, as the soft, whispery sounds of the wind through the open cornfields muted to nothing more than a tinny echo. The darkness was near absolute, save for a faint glimmer of starlight peaking through a hole in the roof, its light little more than a beacon above whose luminance was swallowed by the structure's expanse.

*Deep breaths, Walker. Just a few moments more*, I told myself, inhaling a lungful of air rife with the scent of earth and decay. It's what I imagined the inside of a grave smelled like.

"Guys!" Lydia said, and mine and Sam's flashlights zeroed in on her; a coalescence—like the watchtowers finding their fleeing captive. She was pointing her own flashlight at the silo's wall.

"What the fuck?" Sam said, but my mouth had gone too dry to voice a similar statement.

Quotes and taunts covered the metal wall; things like *Old Man Moody's going to get you, Die, bitch, die, Watch the flames, and Burn, burn, burn*, to name a few, accompanied by drawings of pentagrams and devils.

I was short of breath, the repetitive whooshing trickling to shallow gasps. I placed my index finger on my neck, checking my pulse: my heart was racing.

Lydia moved closer to the wall, tracing the words and images like a detective with a blacklight looking for signs of bodily fluids. Considering the color of the graffiti, I didn't think a discovery like that would be much of a surprise.

*How did I let myself get into this situation?*

*Because you want her to pay*, replied a tiny voice buried

deep in the middle precentral gyrus of my brain. *Don't deny—*

*Quiet!* I thought, wishing I could scream it at someone, that my brain was a person so I could beat it into submission to stop this assault on my senses. I felt an amused rumbling in my gut, and then the feeling passed just as quickly as it had come.

*Fuck.*

"Don't follow the lights," Lydia was saying.

I couldn't help myself. "Yeah, okay, Sméagol."

She sighed loudly. "Very funny, Walk, but it says it right here. It must mean the Moody light. And the lettering, it looks like—" Lydia cut off, jumping backward away from the wall. Sam hurried to her side, placing an arm around her shoulders protectively.

"What is it?"

"We need to go, Sam. I've seen enough."

"Lyd, seriously, what did you see?"

"The letters, the phrases, all of it," she said, sweeping her hand in a gesture to encompass all of what was in front of them, "I think it's blood. Look at the coloration for God's sake."

"Come on, Lydia, this isn't funny."

"Do I look like I'm in a joking mood?" she asked, piercing him with glaring side-eye.

"N-no, I'm just...I'm freaked out, okay," he said and grabbed her hand.

There it was, the poorly worn mask of their platonic relationship finally being stripped away. I knew I'd been right about them fucking.

They didn't break apart, looking at me as if to gauge what I thought. Jealousy bubbled up to my cheeks; they felt hot.

"I already assumed that was dried blood," I said haughtily.

They both looked taken aback. Why had I said that?

"Yeah, okay, well then you should be fine with us getting the fuck out of here. Let's go, Lyd," Sam said, leading her toward the jagged hole in the side of the silo.

"Sam, I—" But my protest wasn't enough. They were gone. "Shit."

I hurried after them and struggled to keep up. I could feel the claws of irritation digging into me, trying to force another reaction out of me for the unfairness of being relegated to an afterthought by my two best friends, but I wouldn't let it take hold. I was probably in this mess for behaving like an asshole, something a boyfriend or two had been more than happy to accuse me of to justify our breakup.

When I reached the truck, Sam and Lydia were already buckled in. Lydia glanced at me and gave me a half-hearted smile.

"Sorry about that back there."

She shook her head. "It's okay, Walk. Sorry we didn't tell you about this," she said, lifting her hand that was entwined with Sam's on the armrest.

"Please, I'm happy for you both. I shouldn't let my bitterness on dating take away from that."

Sam grunted in agreement and turned the key in the ignition—good ol' Sam with his eye on the prize: getting the fuck out of there. The engine started to turn over in a concerted effort, with sputtering and rumbling fits, before ultimately quitting, as if it was too tired to carry on.

Sam smacked the wheel and tried again, turning the key with fervor, his body bouncing on the seat as if his own movement could somehow funnel its kinetic energy into the damn truck to make it work, but, as to be expected, it was folly.

"What the fuck, what the fuck, what the fuck!" He yelled, and my insides burned with the same sentiment and rising panic. Lydia's breath quickened, her wide eyes locking onto mine, reflecting my emotions back to me like a mirror: pure terror.

A loud pop, followed by an immediate slant to the truck, jolted me. Lydia screamed.

I looked out my window, searching, trying to find something to home in on. I was like an auditory bloodhound, my eyes rather than my nose pursuing my target. I opened the door and climbed back out, despite Lydia and Sam's hysterical shouts; I needed to know. I froze in place like Han Solo in carbonite when my eyes caught sight of the radial slash, a perfect incision leaving the rubber as nothing more than a flaccid scarf around the gleaming silver ornament of the rim.

I heard more screams and then time accelerated; it all happened so fast. Hands grabbed me, pulling me along. It was Sam, Lydia was in front of us, and, while running, their words were indecipherable. The light, that burning orb of fire they claimed was Old Man Moody, was back, hovering over the road and racing toward our vehicle. It was colossal, larger than the truck, polluting the air with the hot smell of scorching wood and plastic.

"Get in," Sam yelled, his words muffled as he pushed me over the sharp opening in the side of the silo, plunging us into darkness, save for our silhouettes, backlit by the raging form of the Moody light.

More screams, and in that split second, my world was ripped asunder.

TIME RIGHTED ITSELF, slowing to its natural rhythms, sharpening into focus from the flurry of scenes my mind had cycled through, as if my life was being played on an old-time projector whose film slipped, then got back on track.

Lydia was cradling Sam in her arms, rocking back and forth, her face contorted in tearful sorrow.

"It will be okay, Sammy. It will be okay. Please stay awake. I love you. Don't close your eyes. Please, Sam, open your eyes. You can't leave me...Please."

Her pleas went unanswered in the haloed glow of her phone's flashlight, illuminating them at an off-kilter angle from the ground. I could hardly discern the scene, but I saw enough: the gushing, arms-length slash down Sam's thigh —his femoral artery, or so I assumed—blood pumping out of him in pulses like a carton of milk that had been toppled over, air forcing its way into the container to force out the liquid. His face was pale, the life leeching out of him.

I was frozen. The sight of the large flap of severed skin fluttering under his gushing blood like a buoy adrift in a storm at sea, exposing the inner meat of his leg, destroyed me. Something snapped within me, my reality becoming untethered. He was my best friend; mine before Lydia came along, and he'd never turned his back on me, never leaving me to fend for myself. Who was I without Sam?

Lydia's mouth was open in a soundless scream, her

hands, trying to hold Sam's leg together, drenched in the bright red of death as she rocked him. Sam's eyes were open, devoid of life, replaced with an eternal blankness.

*No!*

I glared at Lydia, fantasizing about throttling her—the very sight of her made bile rise in my throat. Lydia didn't deserve to hold Sam; it should have been me.

*This is your fault, you bitch,* I thought. My hands shook as I struggled to maintain control. Why couldn't I stop the surges of resentment? I didn't know what was happening to me, but I needed to act; one of us had to do *something*.

"I'll get the backpack. Sam said he brought provisions. Maybe there is something that will help," I said, my voice distant to my ears as if spoken in a dream.

I was desperate. I wasn't a doctor and certainly couldn't repair a filleted leg, but I also couldn't sit there watching one friend cradling another—my best friend—and do nothing.

Lydia didn't even acknowledge me before I ran to the opening in the silo and climbed over the jagged metal dripping with Sam's blood, the liquid remnants of my best friend. I pushed the image out of my mind, not letting myself get sucked into the cyclone of sorrow that surely would pull me under into the depths of despair.

The night air hit me, crisp and icy, and I returned my focus to the matter at hand. I expected to see the Moody Light, or the charred remains of the truck, something to justify the mad sprint to the silo that had resulted in my friend's death, but all was still, even the breeze, and the truck was where we'd left it, doors wide open, no worse for wear. Even the moon had started to glow again; the cloud cover had passed.

*I must be hallucinating*, I thought. Certainly something should be waiting for me, or the truck destroyed or—

I swiveled to peer back into the silo's innards, and the weight of my loss came crashing back down, after that infinitesimally brief reprieve. Lydia still rocked Sam in her arms, her hoarse whispers distant in the echo chamber she knelt in.

"Sam...Wake up. You have to wake up..."

I closed my eyes. I couldn't look at her, couldn't see him again like that. But I needed to, didn't I? We couldn't leave Sam here. We needed to take him home, tell his parents. What would we say to them, to other people?

We'd probably get arrested. Nobody would believe we saw a ghost, or a fireball, or whatever the fuck was happening on Moody Road. We deserved it. We should have left before coming to the silo so that Sam wouldn't be taken from me, from Lydia.

*No—Lydia deserves this. She deserves the loss of her lover for pushing us, the slut.*

I inhaled sharply at my simmering anger, a match just waiting to be struck within me. I tried to swallow the pain and growing resentment, reminding myself that we'd all agreed to his little adventure, but I was starting to lose control of myself.

A breeze tickled my skin, carrying the smell of burning rubber and leaves to my nose. I opened my eyes, my fury unchecked. I'd had it with that fucking ghost and this gripping fear that kept handicapping me. I embraced my rage, that white-hot teenage conflagration of insecurity, invalidation, and toxicity that maturity held at bay like a wet Band-Aid—a mere covering that the slightest application of pressure would expose in the best of times.

I followed the scent, pivoting toward a shadow that

continually stretched from its place of origin to my right by the glow of the again-exposed moon overhead. *That's the shadow again!*

I let history repeat itself, diving headlong into danger and recklessness that was the highlight of my high school tenure, stumbling across the grass toward the old house and the tree where something dangled from its gnarled branches.

My steps were slow and uncertain, like wading through water on the shore, but I didn't let that deter me, nor did I blanch at the flickering candle lit in the top-floor window of the house, a beacon signaling me to follow. If I were thinking clearly, I would have asked who'd lit it or how the large, body-shaped mass had been hung on the tree, but I did neither. I had a singular focus, and it was to cause pain with my fists to whatever I could find—my father's form of justice.

"Ahhhh!" I bellowed as I reached the tree, lunging forward and grabbing the dangling form, pulling it to the ground. My body crackled with hate, my teeth clenching until I heard my jaw pop as I pummeled the form again and again, the skin of my knuckles on my right hand splitting in the midst of my onslaught.

*This is for Sam. For Sam. For Sam.* "For Sam!" I yelled with that final blow, falling backward with exhaustion, the fight leaving me. Much as it always had been, my anger only fueled me for so long before the adrenaline wore off. My body was spent, weak, like I'd run a marathon, and I let my head hit the grass. Tears welled, the barricade I'd erected in my mind collapsing, and I started to weep, the candle still flickering in the window above, taunting me.

"Fuck you," I muttered, wiping my eyes with my sleeve. I steadied my breath, trying to suppress hiccups, and sat up.

Now that my anger was released, I realized I needed to get back to Lydia; she couldn't handle Sam alone.

I turned on my phone's flashlight and directed its beam on the shadowed mass near my feet.

"What the—?"

It wasn't a corpse or anything so gruesome, but a potato sack, split in various places from my flurry of blows, spilling its contents of corn husks and hay onto the grass. How hadn't I noticed that, and where did it come from? Sam and Lydia had circled the tree before. That meant somebody was there with us and had hung it up when we weren't looking. While I couldn't explain the Moody light, there was no other explanation for the sack. I looked toward the house again, toward that lit candle in the top-floor window...somebody had lit that, too. The flame winked out as I was staring. The hairs on my arms stood on end.

The whole facade of the house was as black as a fresh patch of asphalt, the shadows of it on the ground matching the jagged gothic forms I'd seen earlier, an impossibility based on the house's traditional square-box shape.

"What the fuck is happening?" I whispered. It wasn't natural.

If someone was there to answer me, they'd chosen action over words to give me a response. A scream pierced the silence, like a ball shattering a pane of glass, and I whipped my head around to face the silo, its hollow shell amplifying the sound like a megaphone, sending the shrill noise out into the night in an echoey cacophony.

"Lydia!"

I'd left her alone in a haunted place, cradling the corpse of my best friend as if a dilapidated grain silo was some kind of haven. I hadn't even thought twice, driven by my emotions, my anger. I started running to her. She was my friend too—my last remaining friend. Why had I done that?

*Because you blame her.*

I recoiled as if slapped, stopping in my tracks. How could I think something like that? But then again, it must be true—what other explanation was there? I'd been waging an internal battle all evening, despising her one moment and pleading for her forgiveness the next. But was it really how I felt, or was it this place; was it Moody Road?

"I'm coming, Lyd!"

I hopped over the jagged entrance, its serrated edges an old acquaintance at that point, painted in Sam's blood, and landed in the barren interior. Nobody was there to greet me; the place where I'd left my friends was empty save for a large circle of blood-saturated dirt and Lydia's phone, its flashlight on.

"Lydia?"

There was no response, which I'd already known there wouldn't be. I wished it was all some big joke where she'd pop out with Sam from some corner and say, "Just kidding, here we are!" But it wasn't a practical joke, and there were no corners for her to hide in, with it being in an empty circular space. It was me alone against whatever that thing was; me alone, as I'd always been, with no champion to love or seek protection from, everything I'd missed growing up with a father like mine—it was my biggest fear.

I'd spent years hiding behind Sam and Lydia, holding to them as a fallback to absolute loneliness. When I'd been outted, I became the only openly gay kid, and was nearly shunned by my parents, saved only by a sister who'd had an abortion—it turned out my dad couldn't handle excommunicating both of his kids, otherwise his whole legacy would have been a waste. But just because they didn't throw me out on my ass, it didn't mean I hadn't lived in fear of their ridicule or their judgment on a daily basis.

The thing was, I knew that would happen if I lived my truth, and I did it anyway, though it was that boy in eighth grade who gave up the game. That led to years of rage that I tried to keep in check that ultimately burst out as I'd stormed out of the silo—a release that didn't even feel cathartic because, as a result of leaving them alone, I'd lost the two people I cared about the most.

"Lydia. I'll find you."

Skirting Sam's blood, I picked up Lydia's phone and waved its light in a sweeping arc along the walls. Whoever grabbed them—her scream was evidence enough of an assault—didn't come in the way I had. I would have seen them, which meant—

I stopped short as the flashlight seemed to be swallowed in a small fissure in the wall opposite me. I stepped closer and was able to make out the details of an outline on the wall where a piece of metal was adhered except for a gap that was exposed to the outside. I nudged the piece with my shoe, and a whole panel of the wall fell over, exposing a roughly six-by-three-foot hole in the side. I peered through, my gaze landing on the shadowy outline of the house.

"Gotcha."

I didn't hesitate, squatting down to clear the sharp upper edge of the metal opening and stepping out on the backside of the silo, though this time clearheaded to my circumstances and what was at stake: saving Lydia.

I pointed Lydia's phone at the ground and caught a glistening trail of blood in the flattened grass. I swallowed the bile that rose in my throat and ran, following it. I didn't question where I'd end—of course, it would be the house. It was always meant to be the house.

The blood trail stopped at a pair of storm doors, the kind that lie flat on the ground and people pull up on to access the basement, like I'd seen in one too many movies of people fleeing tornadoes. They were wide open, an inky-black maw waiting to swallow me whole and deposit me into its depths.

I hesitated as my rational mind caught up to the emotional rush I felt to save my friend. I knew something was waiting for me down there, I'd followed its trail—but what choice did I have?

I peered over my shoulder at the barely perceptible outline of the truck whose engine wouldn't start and whose tires were shot. Despite the folly of it all, I could feel the vehicle tugging at me, calling to me to save myself. I was on the precipice: I either pulled back from the ledge and returned to the truck in hopes of getting it working or took the plunge into the house, hoping for the best.

I won't lie and say I wasn't frozen in indecision for a few moments, because I was, wondering how far even my feet would take me if need be. But I couldn't abandon Lydia to whatever or whoever had grabbed her, and I wouldn't leave Sam's body behind to be tossed in some unmarked grave. I would find my friends and get them out of there.

"Fuck." Why did that have to be the time I decided to be noble?

I jumped, and not metaphorically; I actually leapt through the opening, needing the momentum to shake myself out of my lethargy, but I stuck the landing with only minimal discomfort to my ankles—not too bad in the full dark.

I pointed the flashlight beam in front of me and tried to

get my bearings. I was in an old cellar, the walls stained and peeling, whole chips of paint flaking off in various hues of rusty orange, red, and brown. The air was humid and oddly warm considering the chill outdoors. It smelled of must and rot. I held my breath, fearful of breathing in spores, but realized there wasn't a point to it and quickly abandoned the effort; I wouldn't last down there for more than a few seconds—I'd never been good at going underwater for a reason—and switched to taking shallow breaths, unable to do any more than that even if I tried because the strong smell forced a reaction like I'd had at my Nana's house when I caught a whiff of mothballs. I wanted to puke.

All of the stimuli were a lot to take in at once, and only when I felt water seep into my shoes was I spurred into action. Like the air, the ankle-deep water, murky and thick like mud, was warmer than it should have been. Why hadn't I heard a splash when I landed?

I needed to be more cautious going forward, but time was of the essence. I just hoped a drop that would suck me under wasn't hidden beneath the sludge; the consistency was too thick for me to have any hope of swimming out.

I trudged on. I only moved a few steps before I began to despair, exhaustion weighing on me. A thumping that started in my temples seemed to vibrate down my body through my legs, a thudding noise sounding in my ears with each step.

*Thud.*

I felt a ripping sensation in my core, an emotional wound splitting open to expose its infected pus-filled meat to the fetid air. I stumbled, my vision going black before shaking myself back to consciousness. I burped, the taste of vomit on my tongue.

I took another step forward.

*Thud.*

Our lips were wet against each other, me and the other boy, my eighth-grade kiss, the culmination of so many desires I'd had since those first stirrings in my crotch as a boy. The shirtless men in store advertisements being nowhere close to the warmth of his erection against my leg, a pulsing matched by my own. The gasp for breath before the door opened, the shove backward, the fright in his eyes, followed closely by a decision, a steeliness that I didn't understand until his angry frown matched those of the other boys standing behind him.

"Get off me, faggot! He pulled me into the closet and tried to touch my dick and then kissed me. Walker's a fag!"

The first cut.

*Thud.*

My dad threw open my door, a crackling energy surrounding him like thunder clouds. I knew that look he wore; we all did. Mr. Hollier-Than-Thou was on a rampage.

"Walker! What the fuck is this I hear about you with another boy? Is it true? Well, is it?"

The intensity of his eyes, smoldering hatred that I knew all too well in those moments when I myself lost control, the one true inheritance I'd gotten from my father, stole my breath. I could feel the heat on my skin under his gaze, as if he was spearing me with jets of flame from his eyes.

"Dad, I—"

"Spit it out, goddammit!"

He raised a fist, the vein in his forehead protruding, a pipeline ready to burst, but he stayed his hand—the guillotine primed to fall.

"If it wasn't for your sister and her *mistake*, your ass would be on the street. I'd better not hear anymore about this again, you hear?"

He was gone before my quivering lips could form a response.

The second cut.

*Thud.*

Sam put his arm around my shoulder, trying to reassure me.

"She's new to town, man, don't be like that. She's really cool."

"Lydia? What cool person is named Lydia?"

"Because Walker is any better?"

Sam cringed. He hadn't said that; a girl had. She was small in stature, but carried herself with a confidence that demanded respect, surprising for a fourteen-year-old in our town and something I, oddly enough, felt I needed to give her.

"Sorry," I mumbled, and she nodded in approval.

Sam beamed as if the exchange between the new girl and me conveyed acceptance. I could already see he was besotted with her, and I felt a stab of jealousy like a knife sliding between my ribs.

*I'm going to lose him to her. I'm*—The third cut.

"No!" I yelled, my breath heavy, and the memory shattered. There was a rumble in the distance, tiny waves forming on the murky sludge at my feet—it sounded like a wolf's growl. I held still, trying to be as quiet as possible in hopes of hearing more—I had certainly heard that wrong. A wolf?—before thinking better of it and trying to move faster.

There was something about this place. It wanted to dredge up memories, trauma I'd long since gotten over or at least squirreled away deep in my psyche beneath layers of artifice and validation. Was this Old Man Moody? Why would he be doing this?

As if in response, I felt a jolt of pain, not a direct sensation of my own, but the awareness of it, traveling through the air on a current like static; the air crackled.

Memories circled in my mind, a flipbook of images whose pages turned so quickly the pictures began to move, tightening their noose of melancholy around my sense of self, a cinching belt around my neck.

"I can't let them—Ah!" I clutched my head, still moving forward, one foot in front of the other, ignoring the whispers of past boyfriends, my father, and old acquaintances who taunted me, who told me I'd amount to nothing.

I wouldn't let myself be sucked under; I remembered my friends.

"You got this, Walk," Sam had said when I told him I'd applied to college even though I was a C-average student. I wouldn't become my father. I'd move on from the country towns of my youth to a place that would accept me, and I'd find someone to love.

"We love you, Walk. If anyone's got enough fire in them to make something happen, it's you," Lydia had said…Sweet Lydia, my friend.

The flashing memories stopped, and another growl sounded in the distance. I'd won that round with the fucking demon.

I scaled the refuse floating about in my path and reached a flight of stairs. I had no confirmation that I needed to climb them, but the weight of the sorrow in the air, dense like the moisture on a humid day, increased the closer I got.

I ascended to the first floor, and the darkness of the basement behind me became nothing more than an afterthought.

IT WAS as if I'd stepped back in time and was seeing the remnants of a life all about: wooden chairs and tables, handcrafted dolls, and thick woven fabrics half decayed. Everything was in disrepair, forgotten; it was like an archaeological site, the treasures matching those I'd only seen in frontier museums. My nana's own antiques, passed down from her mother and grandmother, were in far better condition and looked far more modern than what was scattered around me.

A light flickered to life around the corner to my left, casting dancing shadows about the room. A figure moved, or at least its shadow did, feminine in its proportions. Could it be?

"Lydia?"

I followed the path of the hall, looping around the walled off stairwell to the cellar into a room with a large stone hearth. The embers in the fireplace glowed through the cast-iron gates in evidence of recent activity. *Someone has been here…But where have they gone?*

I looked around. The floors were weathered, the wood splintered and blackened by age, and the water dripping down the walls, whose wallpaper was peeling, the adhesive clumped and flaking on the moldy plaster surfaces. The room was sparsely furnished, just a leaning side table, the wood rotted, and an overturned bench that resembled a church pew more than anything else, large chunks missing from its sides as if an axe had been wielded against it.

A single candle placed in a wall sconce illuminated the room, revealing the scene to me, its flames precariously close to a strip of the wall's decorative paper. The wax was hardly melted; it was newly lit.

I placed my hand in front of it; the flame righted itself, stopping its tango.

I didn't feel any airflow, not even a slight breeze on the hairs of my hand, but something had made that candle flame buffet as if in the wind prior to me putting my hand near it.

I lowered my hand. The flame bent again and flickered, its tip pointing toward the fireplace like a compass needle. I looked in the opposite direction from where the flame pointed, assuming the laws of science and airflow applied, and spied another stairwell. This one led up to the next level of the house, with the first few steps visible and the rest hidden by a veil of shadow.

I raised my cell phone, pointing its flashlight upward. The beam of light melted away, as if the stairwell was a black hole, pulling all illumination into itself and unmaking it out of existence.

"Shit," I said, knowing I had no other choice but to carry on. I placed my foot on the first step. Something moved above, reflecting my light back at me. Startled, I dropped my phone as the faint outline of two orbs appeared like a cat's eyes in the dark before winking out.

*Thump.*

*Crack.*

The noises of my phone falling were as loud as gunshots. I looked to the candle, my sole point of light, and it just as readily extinguished in a puff, as if blown by a great wind, blanketing me in the color of my fear: a never-ending black nothingness.

My lungs seized to the point of no air coming in. My nostrils were blocked; something thick and slimy tried to make its way into them, and the cartilage of my nose popped with the force of it.

*You reap what you sow*, a voice whispered, the tone a raspy hiss. It was alien in tone, yet familiar in its message, my ears itching as a squishy, wet piece of flesh caressed them. Was it its tongue—the devil tempting Eve with its serpentine flicking?

*Thrum.*

The slimy mass squeezed a bit further, inching its way in like a worm. The sensation pushed beyond pain, becoming numbing, euphoric even, nearly lulling me into a stupor.

*Don't lose focus. Don't let it in!* I protested.

*Walker*, it hissed, slow and alluring. My mind went blank.

*Thrum.*

"I don't want to be alone," I said before kissing my boyfriend on the lips. There was a distance to him now, our fights being too frequent lately. He drew back, assessing me.

"I can't do this anymore, Walk. You are all lovey and affectionate now, but then what? I don't agree with you or validate you at the right moment, and you flip out? You know, like your father. I can't anymore; I won't."

Each question—each accusation—was like a knife cut, leaving me raw and exposed. He knew how hard it was for me to keep my cool under an assault like this, and I could feel my face growing hot.

"No, wait, you don't get it. Look, I'm sorry, okay. Let's not fuck this up. We're good together."

"Says who? This isn't a negotiation, Walk. I think we should just part ways civilly, like grown-ups."

I felt the vein in my forehead start to throb—just like my father's.

"Are you saying I'm a child?"

"Jesus," he said, throwing up his hands.

The movement struck a nerve—how dare he wash his hands of me after I tried to apologize—and I lashed out, not thinking through my words or what reaction they'd bring; another example of me being a chip off the old block.

"Fuck you!"

"And that right there is why you are alone, Walker."

*But you don't have to be anymore. We could be together*, the voice hissed, the sound a disembodied bubble floating from one ear to the next.

I gasped, slapping at the slimy mass in my nose with one hand and bending to pick up the phone I'd dropped. Its flashlight still on, I thrust it out in front of my body like Frodo in Shelob's Lair with the Phial of Galadriel from *The Lord of the Rings*.

In an instant, my nose felt empty, the phantom feeling of it being stretched out still remaining, but there was nothing there, nor was there anything behind me or in front of me.

Rage roiled in the air, but it was just shy of tangibility. I exhaled.

"Keep the fuck away from me," I yelled, my voice hoarse.

I heard a door slam above, taking with it the bubble of cold that froze me in place. I followed the noise, batting away the tendrils of despair that had tried to make purchase on my psyche.

I reached the landing, looking from left to right. The second floor was small, a series of doors, all shut, the furthest one glistening with a long, dark streak that ran down its length, ending at the doorknob. I didn't need to approach it to know what it was, but wondered—who did it belong to?

*Come in and find out*, the guttural voice whispered. I didn't want to give it what it wanted, but what if Lydia was in there? Or Sam's body, for that matter?

The walk to the door was too easy. There were no further voices, no jellylike quality to the air, just a normal approach with the blood on it becoming ever more distinct in color.

I grasped the knob. It was cold and sticky; it was probably the blood.

"Here goes nothing."

I turned it. Silence. Not just the quiet of an empty house, for even that has the noises of existence: the creaking of the foundation, the dripping of water, the patter of critters escaping the cold night. No, this silence was absolute, like a sound deprivation tank.

I called out, feeling my mouth move—nothing. I didn't even hear the whooshing of my heart in my ears, which was a shock considering it felt as though it would burst out of my chest. I didn't have time to dwell on it, though, as flames burst forth in front of me—a massive ball of them, rotating on its axis like a miniature sun, banishing every shadow, revealing charred bones and pulverized mounds of flesh in the corners.

I screamed again and again, but the result was the same

as when I'd entered the room; my mouth moved, but nothing else.

*You belong with me, here,* the voice said in a raspy tone like that of a smoke inhalation victim. *You're mine.*

The spectre's voice trailed away, leaving the confines of my head to join the roaring inferno. It turned toward me—a brighter flare of white centering in front of me—hungry for my fear and despair.

I threw myself backward out of the still-open door, landing hard on my right shoulder. The flames, a crackling maelstrom of anger and violence, howled at me from beyond the threshold.

*Thrum.*

A girl ran down the hallway. Her screams were for naught: There was nobody around for miles, and her mother and brother were already dead on the floor downstairs, their bodies staining the floorboards. Chunks of her mother's brain matter stuck to her heels.

*Clack, clack, clack.* The boots of her pursuer, like the hoofbeats of an angry steed, out of control, galloping toward her, intent on crushing her in its madness.

She grabbed the doorknob to the room. She could lock the door and bar it until her father returned home, keep herself safe, and tell him what transpired. But it wasn't meant to be, the thought leaving her head as her pursuer got a hold of her and forced it out by the sharp point of the knife that pierced her back, exiting through the center of her chest, silencing her forever.

"My God," I whispered, coming back to myself. The ball of flame burned brighter. It was out for blood, and the crackling howl was like a raging wildfire, intent on consuming me. I held my breath as a blast of hot air engulfed me, certain that moment would be my last, before the door blew closed with a loud thwack.

It was silent again, save for my racing breaths and the sound of my beating heart.

What the actual fuck? Had I just seen Old Man Moody's daughter die?

I knew it had to be that. She'd been trying to reach the room that contained the fireball. Based on my brief glimpse of the hallway, of the angle of the last flight of stairs heading up, I knew that had to be the room.

"But what does this have to do with me?" I asked aloud.

As if in response, the door flexed outward, the boards of it creaking as if it might burst, before the wood settled back to its normal position.

That room was a dead end. I wouldn't be going back in there. I felt a tug of the upstairs, like a string, pulling on my chest toward that final flight of steps, and knew that the only direction I could go was up.

As I scaled them, I knew I likely wouldn't come down from there. The polluted air with its pungent smell of rotting corpse was nearly suffocating, yet I couldn't resist its allure. I craved the pull it had on me like a drug; it had gotten inside me.

I broke out in a cold sweat. My body didn't feel like it was my own as it moved on its trajectory upward like I was on the lift hill of a roller coaster past the point of no return. Why couldn't I stop myself?

Lydia and Sam, that was why. The clarity hit home as I reached another door, though this time at the top of the stairs. I wasn't leaving them there.

*As if you have a choice*, the raspy voice said, and I knew it was right.

I banished the thoughts from my mind, reassuring

myself that *I* was in control, and opened the door. After what I'd seen so far, I expected any number of horrors, not a still attic filled with cabinets and undisturbed cobwebs, but that's what I found.

Dust plumed up from the floors with each of my steps as I carefully avoided sheet-covered objects of varying shapes, likely old furnishings, creating an obstacle course I had to navigate. My phone's flashlight did little to pierce the darkness, its beam creating a confusing jungle of shadows that made the hair on my arms stand on end.

"Hello?" I called out, my nerves getting the better of me. The last thing I wanted was to get a response—unless, of course, it was Lydia.

*Are you so sure? You had the same resentment I had,* the grinding glass sound of the voice said.

"No," I whispered. I had no resentment. Sure, I didn't want to be alone or isolated like my backward little town made me feel, but who did?

"Walker."

I stopped walking. I knew that voice; it was constrained and barely audible as if the words had been choked out, but I knew it as well as I did the pattern of freckles on my cheeks.

"Lydia!"

I swatted the webs away, knocking over one covered furnishing after another, pushing my way through to where the voice had come from.

"Walk—Walker." Her words were hollow, mixed with a strangled sob.

I came to a halt in front of a wall. She should have been right in front of me. A flicker of light peeked out on the ground where the wall met the floorboards, exposing a tiny gap.

The desperation to save my friend to prove the taunting voice was wrong fueled my lunge forward as I threw my body against the wall, splintering it and falling through to the other side.

It was a small space with a single window just to my right, a candle sitting in it overlooking the gravel road below, where I could see Sam's truck right where we'd left it, as dark and quiet as the silo in the foreground. But the confirmation of that light I'd seen earlier was just window dressing to the display taking up the rest of the space. Lydia was there, crammed into a rusty metal cage that she barely fit into. Its bars, which looked to be made of heavy iron, were bolted to the rafters; I'd never be able to break through. More shocking was that Sam's body was strung up to the left of me, taking up the short wall opposite the window. His arms and legs were streaming out what had to be the remainder of his blood via the fresh wounds made in him by the meat hooks he dangled by.

A howl of pure agony pierced the air, moments passing before I realized that it came from me; that I had fallen to my aching knees.

Sam, my brother, my heart, was strung up like a slaughtered hog. Dead. Gone.

It had been one thing when Lydia came into the picture all those years ago, the Eleven taking away my Mike like in *Stranger Things*, even if, unlike the show, it took years for Sam and Lydia to finally act on the inevitable, but despite that, I still always had access to him. Now, though, he was truly gone.

*Thrum.*

A man fell to his knees, screaming in horror. His house, his sanctuary, had been defiled. There was blood all over the floor leading up to the stairs and on the overturned bench in front of the fireplace, where his wife's body was splayed out, her guts and viscera still dripping onto her grandmother's woven rug, the one she brought with her when she moved to America from England.

The man was frozen, his mind struggling to process the trail of intestines draped across the ground, like a rope leading back to the body of his son, the boy's hand outstretched like he'd been reaching for something, perhaps the cellar door just feet away from him.

The man wailed again; it was bloodcurdling. There was a snap—he'd almost not heard it—and he whipped his head around to face it.

Their maid stood there, her eyes widening in surprise. There was blood on her hands and her dress. His gaze drifted to the knife she held in her clenched fist, which had a bloody chunk of flesh stuck to the red-coated blade.

"W-Why?" he asked, his voice quivering.

Her eyes narrowed.

"I told you what I wanted that time we kissed. I loved you, but you wouldn't get rid of her," she said, flicking the knife toward his dead wife. "I took care of it, though."

The man howled.

I gasped, coming to, choking on saliva that had pooled in the back of my throat. That's who did it. All this time, it had been the maid who had killed Moody's family, and nobody had known. She'd been jealous—

*Just like you. We are the same, you and me.*

"No, I'm not. I'm not like you!"

The room dimmed, the hardly discernible colors surrounding me bleaching out to sepia tones. The voice growled.

*Don't lie. I won't warn you again.*

Lydia sobbed in the cage. She was just a few feet in front

of me but it might as well have been miles; my legs had been leached of their strength.

"Lyd," I whispered.

She looked at me, lowering her hands. They were bloody.

*Now you care? Tell her what you really feel. Tell her how she took Sam from you, how you resent her. How you sent the idea of coming here to your friends, hoping this would happen.*

"No, I—"

*Just like all the rest of the jilted friends and lovers before you, you could feel it, the betrayal, what coming here would do. Admit it. Join us.*

"No, I'm not—"

*Say it. You know you want to. You know what you feel when you see them together, your Sam and her. Speak it aloud, become one with it. Do it, Walker.*

Emotions roiled through me. Guilt and shame for knowing the voice was right, I had been jealous, but also anger and melancholy for not owning my feelings, for not steering my destiny in the direction I wanted. Did I really bring this on my friends? Was this whole situation my fault?

"Walker!" Lydia bit out. She was looking to my right, and I turned to see a shadow limping closer to us, something humanoid and scraggly.

Our surroundings darkened further, morphing from sepia to a classic black-and-white horror hue.

My breath caught. A skeleton became visible before us, hardly any flesh left on its bones, and what did remain was blackened and scabbed with a few dangling strands of hair draped over its skull.

*Say it*, it demanded.

"I said no! I'm not like you!"

Pain, excruciating pain. Lydia screaming. I fell on the ground, holding my mouth, unable to form words as blood poured out of it. My mind reeled, trying to catch up to what had happened.

I'd spoken, and the skeleton moved so quickly I couldn't comprehend its movement as it grabbed my tongue and ripped it out of my mouth. A fresh wave of pain rocked me as the immediate past and nerve memory collided. I could feel my jaw snap, tearing indescribably, and heard a pop as the last threads of muscle separated.

The room swam. I couldn't make sense of the world around me, other than the taste of iron in my mouth. I writhed until a bruising blow stopped me cold, pinning me flat to the floorboards.

*I warned you. All you had to do was admit it.* The voice was like that of grinding metal, completely out of sync with the skeletal form's slow-moving jawbone.

Lydia was gurgling.

*Instead, you lied to me, you coward. So I took care of it for you.*

I tried to call out as I saw the blood sluicing from Lydia's sliced throat, but only guttural grunts escaped my lips. My tears were warm, mixing with the blood coating my face.

The floor rumbled.

*Thrum.*

The man dragged the maid by her hair, leaving whole clumps of it on the floor in the house when he first grabbed her. It had taken him three full handfuls yanked out by the roots before he had a good hold on her.

She screamed, begging him to release her.

"I did it for us. I love you. She didn't deserve y—"

The rest of what she was going to say was silenced as he

punched her in the stomach, knocking the wind out of her. She went limp, no longer fighting, but unfortunately for her, he was fueled by emotion, unsure of what he was even going to do next. The only thing he did know was that he'd have his vengeance.

He stopped at the grain silo and looked up at it. His son had helped him finish its construction just a few weeks prior.

"This will do," he said.

The maid began to whimper. "Please."

"Quiet!"

The man threw open the access hatch on the side of the structure and tossed her inside. The maid tried to catch her balance, hoping to use the opportunity to flee, but the man was one step ahead of her, kicking the side of her leg with as much force as he could muster; her shin shattered like twigs beneath the hooves of a steed. The resulting scream reverberated inside the empty silo.

"You took them from me, you Jezebel. My wife. My children—" he choked up, grinding his teeth to force down his sorrow. "You will answer to the Lord."

The man stepped back outside and grabbed the barrel of lamp oil sitting on his cart. He'd gone to town for provisions, picking up conveniences like oil so his son and daughter could practice their letters at night. Now it would have another purpose.

The maid understood her fate the moment he reentered the silo and struck a match. She held her hands out, pleading.

"Please, Mr. Moody. Don't."

"Did you give the same mercy to my family?"

Her eyes darkened. "Fine, but you killed them. You're

the adulterer. The moment you kissed me, you sealed their fate. You might as well have stabbed them yourself."

"N-No! That's not true. It was a moment of weakness—"

"Ha, you admit it. Murderer."

"No!" He yelled, his voice manic.

He grabbed his hair with his free hand, the guilt and frustration trying to find an outlet. He didn't mean anything by the kiss; it meant nothing. He'd had a bit too much ale one night, that's all.

The maid pounced at the agony on his face. "You may as well have pushed the knife into your daughter's back," she said, sneering.

"Aaargh!"

He hurled the oil barrel at her, the wood splintering against her face and spraying the flammable liquid all around the silo's interior. The maid had known she wouldn't be walking away from what she did, and if that was the case, then neither should Mr. Moody. In that split second before he threw the barrel, she saw the torment on his face, the utter collapse of what made that man whole. He'd never be the same, and that would have to be enough.

He struck a match and tossed it onto her. She immediately burst into flames.

I returned to myself, struggling to catch my breath as the skeleton of the maid leaned in closer, a blackish fluid thick and viscous, dripping from her mouth.

*Now you understand, don't you? Your friend was like Moody's wife: an obstacle. He never forgave himself for his betrayal. He immolated me, you see, trying to cast away the guilt, but I taunted him until the end of his life, when he finally hung himself from that tree.* She laughed. It sounded like nails being shaken in a metal can.

*His spirit was never able to rest, though, still roaming this land trying to burn away the hearts of the wicked like mine, but he can't get me again. But you, you're the bad one now. The jealous one.*

The room started to grow hot, and I could hear the crackling sound of burning kindling. I looked at Lydia lying on the floor. Her blood was still gushing out like a newly breached dam. The maid followed my gaze.

*It had to be done. You wanted it deep down. We needed it.* The maid grabbed a strand of her few remaining hairs and plucked it. *But now it's time for you to join us. Mr. Moody knows the scent. He'll find you.*

The hair hit my chest, and the weight of that single strand was like that of a heavy chain, taking my breath away. The crackle of burning tinder grew deafening, light shining through the gaps in the wall illuminating the skeletal maid in a ghastly glow. Her jaw bones slanted, a sort of smile that relieved my bowels at the sight of it.

She laughed again, slinking away as the room suddenly became as bright as the sun. My eyes watered, the unfiltered magnitude of light too much to bear.

I screamed, praying for death, for an escape from the pain.

Pure whiteness engulfed me.

I DROPPED THE PEN, my hand cramping after my written tirade.

It felt so good to have gotten it all down. I'd gone on and on, the priest having to swap out my notebook for a fresh one halfway through as my tale spilled from me onto the page. His eagerness seemed to match mine. I'd been waiting so long to get my opportunity, hoping I'd finally reach people who would try to understand what happened, no matter how crazy it sounded. Surely a man of the cloth could see that it was possible.

The priest caught my gaze and smiled. It was broad and showing too many teeth as he slid the notebook and pen away from me. I felt a tinge of unease.

*No, it's alright. This is a priest!*

He started flipping through the notebook, his eyes meeting mine over the top of the page.

"This is quite an experience, Walker, but I've heard something like it before."

I sat up straighter, or at least as much as I could, seeing as I was strapped in place. I widened my eyes, eager for him to continue.

"Yes. It was a while back. A man was found wandering in a field not far from here, much as you were. He was quite unwell, but after extensive treatment, he shared his tale. The parallels are remarkable. Maybe you can answer a question he couldn't: What happened after the white light? You ended it in the same place he did."

I reached my hand out, opening and closing it, miming for the pen, but the priest just looked at me.

"You can't answer it either, I see. It'll remain a mystery."

He turned toward the closed door and waved his hand in front of the small window inlaid in it. I frowned. A series of clicks preceded the door opening, and two white uniformed nurses entered through the doorway.

"I'll take these notebooks with me. Perhaps this will give some closure to your family about your mental state. I don't think it will help Sam and Lydia's families, but that is why we have the Lord. He will help guide them through this troubling time."

What was he saying? That he didn't believe me? Even if I could speak, I would have been at a loss for words. How did this happen to me? How did I end up here? I had written it all down for him, omitted nothing.

The priest faced me again and did the sign of the cross before leaning in, his face only a foot or so away from mine. He was close enough to smell; he was rife with the scent of decay, masked by a hint of frankincense.

Flashes, like small balls of fire, flickered in his eyes. I gasped. I tried to move my free hand, but my reaction was too slow; one of the nurses had already grabbed it and was strapping it into place.

"Most take care of themselves in the house, Walker, just like Moody did after he killed me, but you somehow made it this far." The priest's voice transformed as he spoke, going from human to that grinding hiss—the same one I heard on the night that haunts me. It sounded like if a rolling pin was taken to shattered glass, a crunching with each word. "You and that other man who survived, I don't know why Moody didn't burn you to a crisp, but no matter, this is where it ends. It's a shame you didn't get much further."

The priest's mouth was then parallel with my ear, and I could feel that slimy, fleshy sensation from all those months ago again, tickling the soft hairs that lined my earlobe. My eyes darted side to side, the nurses not seeming to hear the change in his voice or see what he was doing to my ear. I blinked rapidly, trying to cleanse the sensations and image away, wishing for the nurses to see those flames dancing in his eyes—something!

*This isn't real. This isn't real!*

"Oh, but it is Walker. You should have hung yourself back there at the house, just like Mr. Moody did, or cut your throat at the very least. The cycle always repeats, you see. It's a hunger that is never satisfied, that yearning for love, for acceptance. That unfillable void—my unquenchable hunger."

The priest pulled back enough for me to see his face, his smile curled into a rictus I recognized, skin pulling tight into a skeletal sneer—the same one that belonged to the creature that took my tongue...that took Lydia and strung up Sam.

I tried to talk, to scream, more than I had in days, weeks —I don't know, as time seemed to stand still in that place —but my mouth released nothing more than the grunts that had become my norm.

The priest stood upright, feigning shock, his face returning to that of a middle-aged man.

"Whoa, hey buddy, calm down!" The nurse to my left said, tightening my body restraint.

*No!*

I fought harder.

"We need a sedative in here!" the nurse called out. "You could have made the end easy for yourself, but if this is how you want to go out, so be it."

"Now, now, we shouldn't frighten him. He knows not what he's doing," the priest said, crossing himself. "In the name of the Father, and of the Son, and of the Holy Spirit. Amen."

His tone was laced with mockery, the final words of the prayer nothing more than a snarl. His face darkened, and his eye sockets were black holes with raging flames at their center.

"It is time to repent, Walker."

The nurses averted their gaze, oblivious; to them, everything was as it should be.

A warden entered and hastily jabbed a needle into my arm. My eyelids grew heavy, dulling my panic, lulling me into the oblivion I fought to escape.

"Thank you for your time, Father. Hopefully, he's making peace with his maker."

"Indeed," the priest said, smirking.

He exited the room as the nurses leaned my bed back to a horizontal position, dimming the lights, and leaving me to drift off into a twilight of despair from which I may never again wake.

MARGO CLOSED her Instagram app and took a deep breath. Of course her two best friends were out having fun together; that seemed to happen more often than not, posting pictures together at bars, parties, and spring break trips, the visual equivalent of rubbing her nose in it.

She knew they loved her; they'd been friends for years, through thick and thin. Whether it was high school drama with boys or hormone-laden arguments with their parents, they'd been through it together. As soon as they went off to college, though, things changed, especially since Margo had to go to the community college near her parents' house while they went downstate to Purdue University.

She missed their times together when it was the three of them, and even more than that, she missed Sylvia.

She knew Sylvia liked men. She'd said as much after they'd had a heart-to-heart one drunken night their senior year that led to Margo coming out—still, thank God, Sylvia supported her. Despite that, she couldn't help her feelings, that stirring in her gut—the butterflies—whenever she heard Sylvia's laugh, or the way her lip quivered with satis-faction when she ate something sweet...it was intoxicating.

Yet since college started, Sylvia had become all about their trio's third: Mandi. Truly, Mandi was no threat, Margo knew, but still—what felt like the endless outpouring of Sylvia-and-Mandi pictures grew maddening. Margo would be lying if she said she didn't fantasize about something happening to Mandi, something terrible, and instantly felt a cloud of despair and guilt for wishing that on one of her best friends all because of her proximity to the one Margo loved, the one Margo couldn't have, at least not in the way she wanted.

Margo sighed and reached her hand out to set her phone on her nightstand when she had a sudden compulsion to open Facebook. The thought took her aback—she hadn't used Facebook in years—but the sensation was too much, her fingers already tapping the app open without her realizing she'd done so, like she'd been remote-controlled or something. Logged in, the app loaded her feed.

"Moody Road? What's that?" she asked aloud, clicking on the post positioned right at the top, the creepy AI-generated graphics of a silo in a corn field drawing her in. She scanned the page. A haunted road, an eerie light—something about it entranced her, reeling her in like a fish with a shiny lure.

*I wonder if...?* She copied the post's link and opened her text thread with Sylvia and Mandi, unprovoked rage building inside of her. She was roiling like a tempest, her vision clouding over as she typed.

> HEY GIRLIES! WHEN ARE YOU BOTH HEADING
> BACK INTO TOWN? I HAVE KIND OF A WILD
> IDEA—CHECK THIS POST OUT! LET ME KNOW
> WHAT YOU THINK!
> XOXO MARGO

She set her phone down, a rush of adrenaline coloring her cheeks, lightheadedness setting in. Margo felt like she hadn't eaten in days, a hollowness churning her insides.

Something tugged at her in the back of her mind, her conscience waving red flags of danger, but she couldn't put her finger on why.

*Maybe it was something I ate.*

Her phone vibrated and she picked it back up. Sylvia and then Mandi had sent their replies.

OMG YES! BE HOME NEXT WEEK!

SAME! CAN'T WAIT!

Margo smiled, her gaze glossing over her reflection in her phone's screen and the glint of red like a dancing candle flame in her eyes.

It was done.

# *acknowledgments*

Thank you to my readers and fellow writers. Your support fuels the font of my creativity.

A special thanks to Sheila Loesch, Kandice Hart, Caleb Thompson, Jordan Chelovich, Rebecca and Adam Allen from Horrifically Well Read, Bled, and Said, Lynn Krueger from @lynnsliteraryadventures, Trevor George, Jonathan Jagdeo, and Mom, my eternal cheerleader.

Last, and most importantly, Justin and Graysen, the two halves of my heart, I could never do any of this without you.

## CONSIDER LEAVING A REVIEW

I hope you enjoyed *Moody Road: A Novella* by Chris Kauzlarich. If you did, would you leave a review? Nothing helps an author more than readers spreading the word so others can discover it as well.

Please use the QR code or website link below to leave a review on Goodreads. If it isn't too much trouble, could you also leave a review at the place where you purchased it? I will be eternally grateful :)

Thank you again for your support, and happy reading!

https://www.goodreads.com/book/show/252074512-moody-road

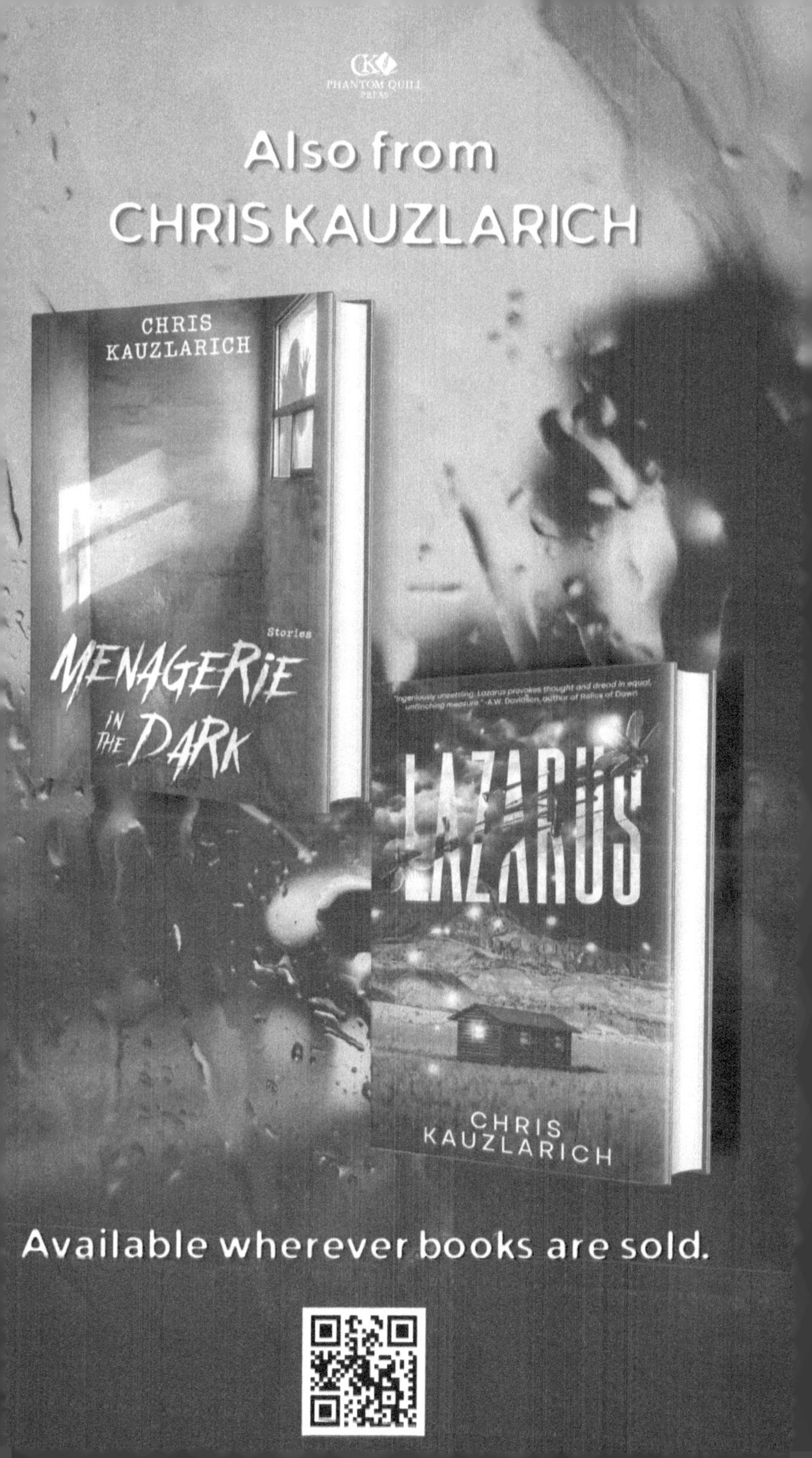

# Also from
# CHRIS KAUZLARICH



## Available wherever books are sold.

Chris Kauzlarich is the author of the horror short story collection *Menagerie in the Dark* and the novellas *LAZARUS* and *Moody Road*. A member of the Horror Writers Association, the International Thriller Writers, the Authors Guild, AWP, and the Chicago Writers Association, he writes dark fiction that unsettles precisely because it lives so close to home. A graduate of Purdue University, Chris lives with his husband and daughter between Chicago, IL, and Naples, FL — or somewhere on the open road in their RV, where the best and worst ideas tend to find him.

To stay updated with Chris and discover new books, connect with him on social media or sign up for his newsletter at chriskauzlarich.com.

facebook.com/Writer.Chris.Kauzlarich

instagram.com/chris.kauzlarich

goodreads.com/kauzlarichcl

amazon.com/author/chriskauzlarich

threads.com/@chris.kauzlarich

bookbub.com/authors/chris-kauzlarich